Maggie Doesn't Want to Move

Elizabeth Lee O'Donnell

illustrated by Amy Schwartz

Aladdin Books

Macmillan Publishing Company   New York

Collier Macmillan Publishers   London

Aladdin Books
Macmillan Publishing Company
866 Third Avenue, New York, NY 10022
Collier Macmillan Canada, Inc.
First Aladdin Books edition 1990
Printed in the United States of America
A hardcover edition of *Maggie Doesn't Want to Move* is available
from Four Winds Press, Macmillan Publishing Company.

10 9 8 7 6 5 4 3 2 1

Library of Congress Cataloging-in-Publication Data
O'Donnell, Elizabeth Lee.
Maggie doesn't want to move / Elizabeth Lee O'Donnell;
illustrated by Amy Schwartz. — 1st Aladdin Books ed.
p.   cm.
Summary: Simon expresses his own sad and fearful feelings about
moving by crediting them to his toddler sister, Maggie.
ISBN 0-689-71375-4
[1. Moving, Houshold—Fiction.   2. Brothers and sisters—
Fiction.]   I. Schwartz, Amy, ill.   II. Title.
[PZ7.02386Mag   1990]   89-37751
[E]—dc20   CIP
                                                   AC

For Al
—E.L.O'D.

For Claire
—A.S.

My sister, Maggie, doesn't want to move.

"Mom," I say, "Maggie doesn't want to move."

"Don't be silly, Simon," says Mom. "I'm too busy to play games."

Maggie and I go to the playground. It's just in the next block.
Maggie isn't allowed to go more than two blocks from home.
There won't be a slide like this one in the new place.

How can Maggie give up a good slide like this one?
Maggie likes the swings, too. She thinks they're neat.
"Maggie," I say, "maybe we should go by school."

Mr. Atkinson is dumping trash. How can he throw all that good stuff away?

"Hello, Mr. Atkinson," I say.

" 'Morning, Simon. I hear you're moving today."

"Maggie doesn't want to move," I tell him.

"Really?" says Mr. Atkinson. "Why?"

"I told her Mrs. Acosta won't be there. How can you go to school without Mrs. Acosta there to smile at you? And tell you it's okay that you got two plus three wrong? And say, 'You'll do better. I promise.'"

I decide we'd better go. Maggie might start crying.

" 'Bye, Mr. Atkinson." I hold out my hand. Mom says always squeeze back when you shake hands. Nobody wants to hold a dead fish.

"Good luck, Simon," says Mr. Atkinson, squeezing back at me. "Maggie will like your new house once she's there."

I shake my head. "No, she won't."

Back at our house, the moving van is outside. It's a
block long, almost. Men carrying furniture go in and out.
They're taking out the couch. And the table. And my bed!

Maggie can't stand it! Billy's mother will have to hide her. No one will look for us there. It's three blocks away. We can hide there forever. Billy's mother makes good banana and honey sandwiches. We can eat banana and honey sandwiches forever.

"Billy's Mother," I say, "Maggie doesn't want to move. Will you hide her? I'll have to stay with her so she won't get scared." Billy's mother looks at me funny. "We won't eat much," I promise her.

"Are you hungry?" she asks.

"Sort of," I say.

Billy's mother lets Maggie in. I don't even have to take her out of the wagon.

"How about toast and honey?" asks Billy's mother.

While Maggie and I are eating, Mom walks into the kitchen.
"I've been looking for you, Simon," she says. I wait to get
bawled out for going three blocks from home. But she doesn't
say anything about it. "It's time to go," she says.

"Maggie doesn't want to move," I tell her again.

"I know," says Mom. She picks Maggie up—smeared honey and all. (Maggie doesn't eat too well yet.) "I forgot that Maggie might be scared of a new place. You're nice to try to help her, Simon, but we have to move."

"Maybe," I say carefully, "she could stay with Billy's mother. I could stay and help her some more."

Mom shakes her head. "What would I do without her? And how could I be happy without you?"

"Yeah," I say. "But Maggie doesn't want to move." I push my toast around.

"I have an idea," Mom says. "Let's show Maggie our new house and the new neighborhood and the new school. If she's still scared, maybe Billy's mother will let her stay."

At the new house, those men are moving our stuff in. That part's okay, but Maggie doesn't like the new house. It's not the right color. And neither is my bedroom.

But there is this huge tree outside my window. The leaves are bigger than my hand.

Mom and I walk along
the edge of the road. I pull
the wagon. I don't think Maggie
likes it. It's bumpy. Where are all the
sidewalks?

I see a bunch of trees and bushes and grass.

"Is that the playground?" I ask. "Maggie likes our
playground better."

"It's not a playground," Mom says. "It's a park."

There aren't any swings. I don't see a slide. Maggie isn't going to like this.

But I see a pond. Some men are sailing boats. I see squirrels and chipmunks. And a big, grassy hill. Maggie likes racing down it.

"Let's go look at the school before it gets too late," says Mom.

The school is different. It's all spread out. Maggie doesn't like it. There aren't any banisters to slide on when Mrs. Acosta isn't looking.

We walk along to a separate building.

My old room wasn't in a separate building.

"There won't be anybody like Mrs. Acosta," I say.

"Maggie won't like anybody else."

"Maybe," says Mom. She knocks on an open door.
A *man* comes out!

"Mr. Paul? This is my son, Simon, and my daughter,
Maggie. Simon thinks Maggie won't like it here. We
wondered if we could visit and see if she'll change her
mind."

"Sure," says Mr. Paul. "But the room's a mess." He looks
at me and holds out his hand. His mother must have told
him about dead fish, too.

"You'll have to watch your sister, Simon. We're making
boats, and there are saws and hammers and nails all
around."

"Okay," I say.

"Hi," says this kid.

"Hi," I say back.

"You coming to school here?" he asks.

I shrug and start to say, "My sister Maggie doesn't—"

"Boy!" says the kid. "Are you lucky! Mr. Paul is the neatest teacher in the whole world! Want to see my boat?"

"What do you think, Simon?" Mom asks outside the new house. "Shall we call Billy's mother and ask her to take Maggie?"

The moving van is gone. All our stuff is inside our house. I look at Maggie. She looks at me.

"I don't think so, Mom," I say. "Maggie doesn't want to move."